CROWS

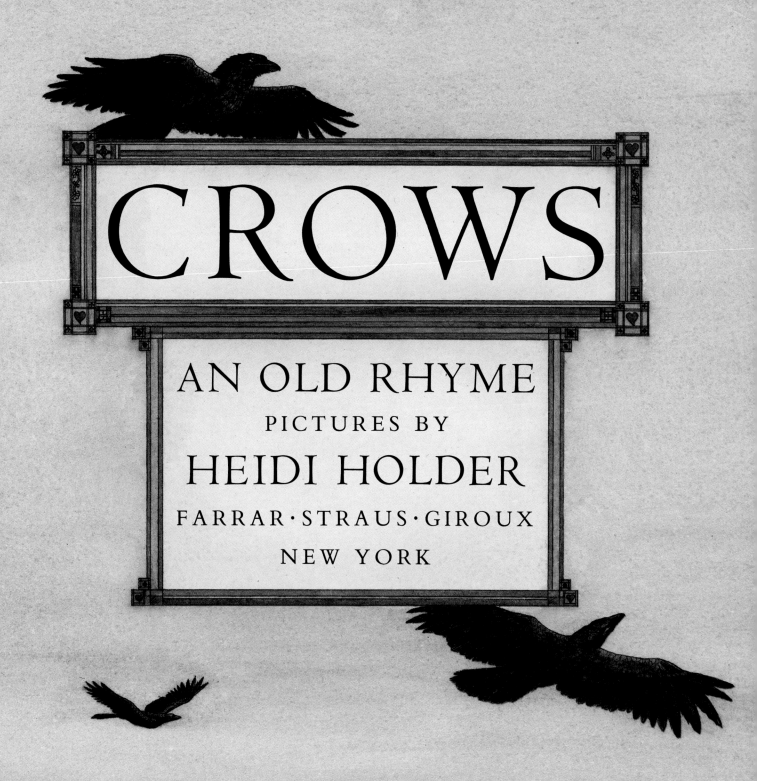

CROWS

AN OLD RHYME
PICTURES BY
HEIDI HOLDER
FARRAR · STRAUS · GIROUX
NEW YORK

Pictures copyright © 1987 by Heidi Holder
Text copyright © 1987 by Farrar, Straus and Giroux
All rights reserved
Library of Congress catalog card number: 87-045364
Published simultaneously in Canada by Collins Publishers, Toronto
Color separations by Offset Separation Corp.
Printed and bound in the United States of America
by Lake Book / Cuneo, Melrose Park, Illinois
Designed by Cynthia Krupat
First edition, 1987

To Eddie

One is for bad news

Two is for mirth

Three is a wedding

F our is a birth

Five is for riches

S ix is a thief

Seven is a journey

Eight is for grief

Nine is a secret

Ten is for sorrow

E leven is for love

Twelve is for joy tomorrow

Notes on the Text

Birds, more than any other creature, are considered prophetic. I first learned of this superstition about crows from my grandfather. The version he knew was originally twelve crows long, but he could only remember the meanings for seven. After researching in the library, I discovered that this folklore about crows began in England and Scotland and was about magpies, not crows. When the English settlers came to this country, I imagine, there were not as many magpies to be found, so they applied the superstition to crows. ❧ I could find no author or authors for the superstition which appears in many versions. After reading these various rhymes, Stephen Roxburgh and I have compiled a twelve-crow superstition which incorporates the seven meanings my grandfather knew, plus five more. I hope it is as close as possible to the old rhyme.

A Few Words about Weasels, Minks and Crows

I once had the unhappy necessity of telling a friend that his heart was as mean and dark as a weasel in a Kentucky coal mine. I was mistaken. The weasel's reputation for meanness is undeserved. He is not mean, merely outrageously sly. Minks are somewhat larger than weasels, but they are of the same animal family and they share many of the same traits as weasels. ❧ Both animals attack their prey with a swift ferocity unmatched by any other forest creature. Their fearless skill as hunters stems, not from cruelty, but from love and devotion to their children and mate, for whom they will tirelessly provide food and protection. ❧ Minks and weasels can never, ever be kept as pets. Their instinct to hunt and kill is too strong, and small children, babies, the family dog, and your feet would unfortunately be in danger of attack. ❧ If minks and weasels seem like barbaric creatures, crows are exactly the opposite. I love crows. They are intelligent, witty, urbane, and cultured, with a highly sophisticated social structure to their flocks. I once saw a young crow, cheered on by his older companions, flying over the rooftops of Manhattan, carrying a whole pizza pie in his beak. ❧ Crows treasure the privacy of their nests and hide them extremely well. There they keep treasure troves of objects they have collected. They like anything bright and amusing, such as tinfoil, car keys, or golf balls. Crows, however, are not sweethearts. I have seen a crow steal two freshly laid pigeon eggs, ruthlessly pushing aside the protesting parents. ❧ I do not think it would be safe to keep a crow as a pet if there are small children in the house, and I am sure the crow would be lonely for his flock. But I have heard they can be taught to talk, and I am sure they would be charming dinner guests.

A Key to the Symbols

Crows	Symbols	Significance
One	Meadow rue	Regrets
	Forget-me-not	True love
	Thistle	Suffering
	Anemone	Forsaken
	Pansy	Thoughts and remembrance
Two	Saffron crocus	Mirth; dispels gloom
	Eight of Hearts	Happiness
	Nine of Clubs	Signifies the absolute certainty of the surrounding cards
	Eight of Hearts and Nine of Clubs together	Gaiety
Three	Pink carnation	Pure love and marriage
	Ivy and bridal roses	Enduring devotion and happy love
Four	A stork	In Northern European folklore, babies are delivered to their parents by storks
Five	A frog	Meeting a frog on the road means you will soon receive gold
	A forked stick of hazelwood	A wand of hazelwood can detect buried treasure
Six	Blackthorn	Difficulties
	A full moon	A time of turmoil
	Clocks	Time is the biggest thief of all
Seven	Six swords	In the Tarot, the six of swords signifies a journey by water
Eight	A white pigeon	If such a bird lands on a windowsill or the roof of a house, it signifies a death in the family
	Solar eclipse	Disaster
	Flies	Sickness
	Spiders	Evil
	Nine of Spades	The worst card in the deck, predicting dire misfortune
	Five-leaf clover	Bad luck

Crows	Symbols	Significance
	Deathwatch beetle	Death
	A black cat	Bad luck
Nine	Yellow acacia	Secrets
Ten	Apple	A symbol of sorrow since the Garden of Eden
Eleven	Flowering cherry	Love, sweet and true
Twelve	A new moon	New beginnings
	Rays of the sun	Happiness and blessings
	Celandine	Joys to come

Acknowledgments

I would like to thank the American Museum of Natural History for granting me permission to sketch from their collection of birds; the unknown artist who designed the fabric I used for the skunk's dress; and Hans Holbein. In designing the lettering for the cover, I based the proportions of the letters on capitals designed by Holbein and reproduced in *Decorative Alphabets and Initials*, edited by Alexander Newbitt (New York: Dover Publications, 1959). The following books were used in preparing the rhyme and as sources for some of the symbols in the paintings: *Credulities Past and Present* by William Jones (London: Chatto & Windus, 1880). *A Handbook of Symbols in Christian Art* by Gertrude Grace Sill (New York: Macmillan, 1975). *The Language of Flowers* (anonymous), copyright Margaret Pickston (London: Michael Joseph, Ltd., 1968). *The Oxford Dictionary of English Proverbs*, 2nd ed., by William G. Smith and Paul Harvey (Oxford: Clarendon Press, 1948). *The Reader's Handbook of Illusions, References, Plots and Stories* by Ebenezer Brewer (New York: J. B. Lippincott, 1880). *Signs and Symbols in Christian Art* by George Ferguson (New York: Oxford University Press, 1954).